THE GRAND DAME OF GRANVILLE AVENUE

The Grand Dame of Granville Avenue

ANNE O'BRIEN

AO Publishing

Contents

*To my Augie without whom I'd lack the courage
and Dr Vogel without whom I'd lack the teeth
Thank you*

Chapter 1

The Grand Dame of Granville Avenue

Rosemary, or Mimi as her friends call her, had become a frazzled malcontent over the past several years and given to spouting "I've had it" out of nowhere which could mean her frequent gripes about Chicago's CTA service or life in general. Every morning after "her shows" she calls her sister, Bunny. Bunny has no answers for Mimi. Bunny is happy going to the Grand Victoria Casino once a week and helping Father Gregory at the rectory. Mimi wants more. She has murky images of regaling "the smart set" with cocktails and witticisms but the 'where' and 'how' have always eluded her. She needs more action and more money. She is tired of pretending she's beyond material yearnings and it's hard to pull off a grandiose image when she is yanking a cart of Aldi's groceries onto a bus and maneuvering it around a dirty backpack.

She often laments to Bunny that life goes by too fast. But life has, in fact, been merciful and patient with Mimi allowing her plenty of thinking time. She'd grown up in a family of smug Irish Catholics. Her father, a Spanish teacher at Sullivan High on Chicago's far Northside entered his classroom every morning in bow tie, sleeveless cashmere vest and a Herringbone tweed sport coat. On Sunday evenings his colleagues, looking preoccupied and dapper would arrive at Ed and May Flannigan's apartment building for an evening of highballs, dinner and discourse on world events. Mimi was mesmerized by the complicated words and the confidence with which they exchanged them. Ed and May, whose parents came to Chicago via Ireland and the farm lands of Nebraska considered the three bedroom flat in Rogers Park with its walnut tea cart and bookcase filled with thrift store classics the pinnacle of success. Mimi and Bunny could play the piano, say the Mass in Latin but had not a scintilla of aspiration.

Neither Mimi's nor Bunny's marriages lasted beyond five years and they both ended up on Granville Avenue, a few blocks from their birthplace. Money was a common topic and as elusive to Mimi as the Blessed Trinity. She would counter Bunny's suggestions by enforcing her stance on jobs.

"I might be broke but I refuse to be called a team member. I need intellectual stimulation. I'm not cut out to sort panties and wear a name tag. If you really knew me you would know that is so out of my realm. Maybe I could work at a little used book store. The kind our dad used to visit."

"All I know is that you've got an itch. At least at the casino we might make money but no, that's below you."

"Bunny, It's not like I sit on my rump all day complaining. I tried teaching catechism at St Gertrude's but I slipped on ice and landed in the hospital. And that tutoring job at that homeless place on Howard Street was a damn fiasco. There were only two kids and a bunch of hyperactive Loyola students who were going to build huts in some god awful place over the summer. I was cold and antsy and wanted to go home and take off my bra."

Mimi was secretly developing a habit not uncommon of her age group. She was building a quasi-social life with strangers. First it was the #155 bus driver and then its passengers. They only had to speak English and be somewhat lucid. It wasn't New York and this wasn't a literary circle from the Algonquin Table but it served a purpose. Lucy McDowell caught her eye because she was reading a book by one of her favorite authors, Wallace Stegner. Over coffee at Dunkin Donuts she expounded not on Stegner but on her mother whom she claimed was "asking for it." Mimi wished later she had not given out her phone number.

Jan Steele was a different sort. With her long gauzy dresses and matted grey hair Mimi associated her with the Woodstock culture of the 60's until she visited her uptown apartment. Her contribution to the art world were quilted wreaths covered in cat hair she was planning to sell at Lunt Avenue's summer art fair. One Friday they met for a cocktail at Stan's on Broadway which is distinguished by a green florescent neon "Lounge' over a tilted martini glass. Mimi left when Jan cried over her murdered ex and fell off the bar stool.

Mo Gebbert and his wife Jo were full of bright conversation on the #93 Evanston bus. Mimi accepted an invitation for coffee and a stroll one Sunday afternoon. They started out on the lake with a stream of long winded opinions on world affairs as if they were on NPR. But heading west towards Broadway Mo suggested the alley. Conversation ceased when their heads began bobbing in and out of garbage cans looking for possible treasure. Mimi pretended she had received an emergency phone call and escaped to the nearest sidewalk. These were the kind of tales she would not tell Bunny. Bunny liked her casinos and her lottery tickets and she was not given to what she referred to as her sister's "stunts." She may have believed that any week her ship was coming in but with people she was wary.

A few weeks after the Gebberts, Mimi met Vivian Manley while waiting for the Michigan Avenue bus (which Mimi described as "more upscale"). She was the kind of person for which Mimi had been searching. Each time they met on the #147 she was involved in something new. On a dismal February afternoon Vivian remarked to

Mimi "Come with me tomorrow and I'll introduce you to some fascinating people."

The next morning Vivian and Mimi met on Lawrence and Lincoln Ave by a statue of Lincoln and twenty pigeons. They took the Lawrence Ave bus east to the Levy Senior Center. Mimi was repulsed as soon as she entered the building. It emitted the greasy sour odor of her grade school cafeteria. Vivian grabbed Mimi's arm and led her to a corner of the room. A stooped, pallid faced man wearing pleated trousers and a shirt with an outdated yellowed collar introduced himself as Felix. He was slow to smile but when he did he exposed two missing teeth. He had an accent Mimi could not identify and as he reached out to greet her she was repelled by the cold liver spotted hand.

Vivian in her usual rapturous state screamed "Oh God! Just wait till you meet Felix's friend, Lydia. She's probably already in the cafeteria."

Vivian helped the withered man to his feet and they proceeded to the cafeteria. Mimi noticed spittle at the side of his mouth and felt faint. Another man later introduced as Herman Patoule minced over to their table. He sat down beside Felix and mentioned an essay he had recently read in some literary journal. Herman had a faint odor of garlic and sweat and his teeth were garnished with parsley. He handed the journal to Lydia who was on the other side of Mimi. Lydia was lean and chiseled, almost elegant in faded jeans and turtleneck. She looked like someone who, at one time would have blown smoke rings from a Dunhill cigarette holder. Another woman who introduced herself as Miriam was speaking passionately in a foreign language. She kept patting her massive bosoms and looking to Felix for validation. Felix kept nodding and chewing his prunes. Vivian was daintily picking at a Parker House roll. She suddenly grabbed Mimi's arm again.

"Is this great or what?" She said in her sonorous voice.

Mimi could not describe her morning as great. The crumpled bodies like piles of laundry horrified her. The loud talking and foreign accents made her weary. But a new lipstick at Target and a martini at five gave her renewed buoyancy. While everyone was shouting at one another Mimi got up, snatched her purse and the back of her skirt that had crawled up her expansive butt, waved at no one in particular and headed for the door. Vivian was behind her.

"You sure as hell aren't leaving." Her face was puffy and contorted from animation. Mimi was intimidated.

"I want to stay but it's my sinuses."

"Forget your sinuses and come back with us to Miriam's place." The bosom lady was waving at them.

Instead of taking the bus the motley assemblage meandered up Lawrence Avenue. They passed the Lawrence bus shelter on Western Avenue where woebegone looking people in overcoats were hovered together like crows and entered a doorway between Sassy shoes and Yoder's deli. Mimi had never been in an apartment above a store. The little place was heaving with fabric. The crimson drapes like the ones in O'Malley's funeral parlor on Devon had tassels matching ones on the lamp shades. The massive furniture was crowned in lace doilies and lead crystal. Tattered Persian rugs were strewn about. Its worn pomposity gave it the appearance of old royalty and its visitors a new found hubris. Herman Patoule looking like a bulldog with his heavy jowls and thick legs had abandoned his cane and was leaning against the mantle discussing Proust.

Suddenly Miriam sprinted towards the kitchen, her breasts pointing the way like a ship's figurehead. She was sweating but energized as though she'd just engaged in a sexual romp. She returned with a dismal batch of cookies in paper cups that tasted like the cookies Mimi's daughter used to make in her Easy Bake Oven.

"Tell me" said Vivian as she followed Mimi to the door several hours later "is this Kismet? All these brilliant minds converging together. Felix, you know, was a professor before retiring."

Mimi tried to keep her composure which was always a daunting challenge.

"Well, Can you beat that?"

She was suddenly yearning for familiar terrain. She sprinted down the two flights of stairs. For once she was disinclined to socialize on the bus and besides, the conversations were steeped in contretemps. Two teenagers were arguing and a lady holding a rotund baby nibbling on Fritos was yelling to someone on her cell phone.

"I'm on Lawrence. What's it to you? No. You're shit out of luck. They don't sell beer at this Aldis"

Back in the comfort of her own apartment with its Sears shears and photos of family she had time to reflect. She called Bunny. "I've had it" She paused as she plucked a whisker from her chin.

"Are you still there, Mimi? I'm watching Wheel of Fortune so out with it."

"I think I'll go to the casino with you, just for the ride, of course."

Chapter 2

Holiday Heart

He was a clean-living fellow, a fact he cherished when all else seemed mystifying. This morning was Christmas morning. He needn't go to Mass because he and his wife, Mary, had gone the evening before. Being a man who adhered to schedules he was at loose ends. He squirmed under the comforter testing his joints. The right hip was somewhat sore, but he offered it up "for the poor souls" and tallied the expected turnout of family that day.

Owen hadbeen married just a few months over a year. Mary slept in another bedroom for several incontestable reasons. She was a thrasher and he slept in the dark. Not to say they didn't often convene on his king size mattress to enjoy the weed Mary purchased in Chicago. He was as happy as he could be and loved her at times so deeply that it alarmed him. But after being a bachelor for twenty years he relished these moments before coffee. Mary was a talker and when he thinks this he always adds "Bless her heart." She is kind and affectionate and he has known her for over fifty years because at one time she was married to his deceased brother. And even now she never ceases to titillate.

Today would be devoted to food and family and he could lounge around till noon unless Mary found some last-minute errands for him."Bless her heart' he thinks as he remembers yesterday's appalling load of groceries, "enough cheese to constipate the entire town", various spreads with disquieting labels and two hummus dips which he hates. She had added sweet rolls even after they had agreed that bagels and coffee cake were suffi-cient. He couldn't help but think of that money going to waste and it bothered him that it bothered him. But dish towels decorated in dachshunds with mistletoe in their mouth and Christmas candles from those "rip off shops spelled with a double P" were anathema to a man who saved gift bags.

His condo was small, square and abrupt yet Mary decorated as if she were still in her capacious slightly decrepit apartment in Chicago. If he had allowed him-self to focus on the numerous Santa Clauses teetering on the bookshelves he was sure he would have a panic attack. And Jesus, he loved her, but the stockings pre-sented another conundrum. Was he to fill the "god damn green one" trimmed in fur? The other had 'O' on it and the other, and this is where he must breathe deeply and exhale gently, was for the cats.

With eyes cast to the ceiling he attempted a quick decade of the Rosary. Thoughts of the coming hours, visitors and all that talking made it impossible. He kept hearing the refrigerator door open and shut and wondered why she couldn't just get "the damn stuff out at one time."

"Merry Christmas, darling." He hugged her. When he saw the flannel "get up" embossed with sequins in the shape of martini glasses he knew she wasn't going to play their usual morning Wordle. He stifled a moan as he beheld a virtual sea of red and green. Dishes and bowls of every size including Santa and Mrs. Claus salt and pepper shakers covered the table. In the center stood a white ceramic shell filled with glass pears and a partridge. Artificial greenery and poinsettias snaked throughout the display and around the chairs. Where had this stuff been hiding? And where was this propensity for holiday glitz lurking while she was reading poetry in between caresses and her Pinot Grigio?

"A lot of work going on there, honey. And where were all these things hiding? " He attempted a chuckle.

"Hobby Lobby, darling and thrift stores. I had them stored in my bedroom closet. Oatmeal's almost ready and merry Christmas to you too, my dearest love."

"I heard the frig door opening and closing. What were you getting out. Just curious.'

"I was having a sort of dress rehearsal to see if I had enough serving dishes."

With that Owen retreated to the bathroom to do his daily Sudoku.

At eleven Mary appeared in something that made Owen blink and grab the back of a chair. He wondered if it was sexy or bizarre for an older lady to wear a white furry skirt up to her ass over a red body suit with green sequined Naughty and Nice across her chest? She was twirling to Mariah Carey and sipping a mimosa.

"Listen, darling. since you must leave by two for Carol Stream why don't we open our gifts tonight when we are alone?" He felt an immediate twinge of panic. All this frivolity portended great expectations. Would she think that the money in a Dollar Tree card was crass? But what could be enough to satiate a woman who has forty Christmas books sitting in a giant red plastic bin and "those fucking Vienna Boys singing up a storm at all hours?"

The guests arrived in two cars with more food. There was a flurry of coats being taken, gifts arranged under the tree and drinks being served. After some deliberation Owen put on a red tie and khaki pants. He would have preferred his comfortable Van Heusen shirt but chose the sweater Mary had purchased, "a god awful itchy thing" with reindeer. Much to Owens relief Mary's daughter, Kate filled her mother's stocking and the rest of the gifts were opened within two hours. The women seemed to talk at once without listening to one another which Owen found astonishing. For someone who had been used to a solitary life he was stunned by all the chatter and the background music of those "damn choirs" but relieved he didn't have to think of things to say. The daughters were helping her clean up as he left for Carol Stream.

It had started to snow, icey snow that meant future problems and he worried over their plans for opening gifts that evening. He fretted as he drove down a street of identical houses until he sighted the one with the Irish Flag. John's home gave him a slight case of vertigo. With its high ceilings and sprawling rooms, it reminded him more of a community center. He loved his two sons, John and Patrick but at family get togethers the conversation could be stilted. Lynn and Clare, his daughters-in-law with their liberal opinions that sounded more like declarations made Owen weary. He had to spend a few moments mentally matching the grandchildren with their ages and grades before asking the dutiful questions. He listened to convoluted stories about volleyball tournaments and gymnastic meets until dinner was served. Theirs was a formal sit down with turkey and its accompanying trimmings as well as some vegan "concoction" for Lynn.

It was snowing "like a bitch" and he didn't make it home until after midnight. Mary was asleep and he worried that she would be mad. He felt bloated and exhausted as he put on his grey flannels. He crawled under his comforter along with a bottle of water and Pepto Bismol, relieved to be alone with his gas. He had just fallen into a reassuring dream of getting laid when his phone interrupted the best part. He never gets calls after nine but tonight his daughter, Charlotte left a text. He expected something imploding with brandy induced felicity but instead it was an unpunctuated vitriolic message concerning her husband. He could not continue reading it. His stomach hurt and his hand shook. He went into the living room and put on ESPN. Mary appeared in the doorway in pjs adorned with dancing martini glasses."I missed you, darling. I hope you had fun. We can do the presents tomorrow."

She kissed him on the head. The warm room no longer appeared cluttered but instead cozy and her voice, a lullaby. He wondered if anyone lived a linear life where one event ended with a lesson learned, every chapter a cautionary tale that rendered profundities. It certainly didn't seem that way to him as he lay against three reindeer shaped throw pillows staring at the tree. His was a hodgepodge of good and bad, of progress and retreat, sorrow and jubilance injected with spurts of tragedy and those soft words during sex that keep one from harry carry. Could it be actually something as crude as booze, the Righteous Brothers and an insatiable libido that produced his progeny? His kids were 70's kids raised on Montessori and indulgence. Yet despite art classes that they couldn't afford, not to mention the usual soccer, ballet and little league he wasn't really sure who was happy and who wasn't.

He studied the tree and took note of the intricate decorations Mary had collected through the years. He knew only one thing for certain; he and Mary loved one another in the truest sense of the word. And for a brief and glorious moment he was swaddled in that wondrous time of childhood.

Chapter 3

Meghan's Rise to Stardom

Meghan awoke in a state of fright. She brushed her hand over her body trying to remember what she wore to bed. The apartment smelled like rotten garbage. It was daylight, broad daylight. "Fuck. I overslept." She could feel a booze induced anxiety attack coming on until she remembered she had the noon to six shift at Circle of Life Vintage. As she watched WGN News images began to slowly dribble down into her frontal cortex. She had met up with Trevor and Lila at Annoyance Theater. Was there a fight? Oh, God yes. What did she say? Oh, Fuck! something about improv being a circle jerk. And then Lila said something mean to her. What was it? She pulls her cat up to her chest. Oh, yes! Lila said she had no self-esteem. And then she took an Uber. But she fell first. Jesus, right there on Belmont Avenue. "Megan, you need to work on self-esteem. Why don't you join a health club?" she had said.

She pulled a long grey sweater over black tights, and to appear less disheveled a black eternity scarf from her mother who frequently reminds her of the importance of "looking smart." The Brown Line was filled with serious hygienic looking people, women with aquiline noses and tiny asses and single men as good as married; a car seat looming above them like hologram images in old photos. She secretly longed for this kind of unruffled man with soft spoken friends who meet for Sunday brunch and have high paying jobs with esoteric titles. Her theater friends are both straggly and stragglers employed in retail and hospitality like splay legged Connor who works at Dicks Last Resort and spends free time fondling his beard and blaming people.

Meghan tells herself and others that her studio apartment above Alamo Shoes is a dream realized and that she is a starving artist. But her place is crawling with roaches and dirty throw pillows. The landlord has tried extermination three times and she is afraid to call him again because he overlooks her late rent. In addition to a weekend program at Loyola University she is taking a sketch writing class at Second City because she has been told she is funny. She has murky visions of Saturday Night Live but has no idea how to get there.

She takes a bagel and cream cheese out of her back pack. After the self-esteem comment she feels self-conscious eating it but reminds herself that chubby girls have made it in theater. Look at Melissa McCarthy. And she doesn't have the time for a serious job because she's too involved with her sketch writing. And look at Tina Fey and that job she once had at the Evanston Y. A smell like burnt vegetables interrupted her reverie and she realized after a swift sniff that it was coming from her.

As soon as she arrived at the store she went to the bathroom and applied a damp paper towel under her arms. The store's owner, Kate was in the back room. A clump of blue hair fell over her right eye as she slammed clothing on the table. Meghan knew this portended a bad day. When she was drinking with her friends, she could laugh at the ongoing contretemps but when she was facing her alone, she cowered.

"Can I help you?"

"I paid too much for this shit. The cashmere has a stain, and this fucking poodle skirt wouldn't fit my Chihuahua. And it would be a big help if you get here a few minutes early sometimes."

Meghan went out to the front and made attempts at rearranging the merchandise. Despite their pristine condition the clothes gave off a subtle odor of sour milk. She had to keep reminding herself that this is but a mere paragraph in her future memoir.

Three middle aged sterile looking women were squinting against the glass either trying to ascertain if the store was opened or if it was worth their time. She could tell by the coordinated outfits they were from the suburbs. They did not enter with the usual polite reticence of first-time customers but with officious fury, ignoring Meghan as they burrowed into the folded sweaters. One of the women seemed especially pernicious. She had a smattering of wiry, stern looking grey hair, a face like stale bread and glasses hanging from a pink leather string. She asked to see a pair of topaz earrings in the jewelry case and then proceeded to pick up and return three rings and two pairs of earrings. Meghan's hand was shaking from last night's booze and her boss's crabbiness. Without so much as a nod they left behind a shamble of sweaters and candy wrappers from the free peppermints.

"Tina Fey, Tina, Tina." she muttered.

"Is anyone out there?" Kate was standing by the curtain that separated the store from the workroom

"No. Do you need me?"

"Self-esteem, Meghan." She was remembering her friends comment again.

"I need coffee. Can you get me a caramel macchiato before I lose it?"

Meghan skittered out of the store like a kicked cat and realized at the corner of Milwaukee and Damen that she wasn't given any money. "Bitch."

The wool eternity scarf was making her wheeze and she wanted to kick a few panhandlers as she contemplated asking Kate for reimbursement. There were several young girls in the store when she returned but instead of looking at the merchandise, they were huddled by the coats discussing a guy. Meghan spent the next few hours brooding over the Starbucks money.

At five Kate tossed Meghan a five-dollar bill. "I'm outa here."

As dusk descended Meghan felt as if she was almost levitating with relief. The customers who stopped in from the train were mostly browsers, her hangover was gone and she had been reimbursed for the coffee which once again put a hold on her resignation. After work, she stopped at Highballs across the street to chat with the bartender, Chris who did stand-up at the Laugh Factory. He had a narrow face with a petulant mouth and a prognathous jawline which perhaps unfairly gave him a look of arrogance and his material was obnoxious. She didn't like him but desperately wanted him to like her.

"Wuz up?" He looked annoyed.

"Not much. I need to be revived. I don't know how much more I can take of that crazy place I work. Jesus!"

He placed a Manhattan in front of her and strummed his bony fingers on the bar waiting for her money. Sometimes the drinks were free depending on his mood. She suddenly felt foolish and slightly nauseous.

She took an Uber to Comedy Sportz to watch her friend, Liz perform with her new improv group, the Dillies.

Liz waved her over.

A blond with a pinched face gave Meghan a quivering smile and looked away but her boyfriend, Justin who had a man bun stood up and hugged her. She was suddenly face to face with John Baluchi's face tattooed across his neck.

Liz was hopping up and down like an Pentecostal preacher.

"Oh, my god! I'm so glad you're here. What do you want to drink?"

Meghan suddenly lost her footing. She didn't know if she wanted to go or wanted friends and her cat needed to be fed. After another Manhattan, she was too comfortable to leave and she was trying to ingratiate herself to Kim, the blond who talked in monosyllables and clutched her phone like a weapon. Justin talked incessantly. He was student at Columbia College taking weekend classes at Second City and starting his "comedy journey."

Meghan didn't agree with the improv motto of "no mistakes" and thought the players too wordy and the scenes confusing but she stayed through the entire show afraid her friend would notice if she left early. Going home she chose the slower but tamer Clark Street bus over the Red line. She sat in the back next to an empty paper bag. Across the aisle were two young men with expensive looking back packs, a sleeping Hispanic man holding an empty plastic food container and an old woman with four Aldi shopping bags. As she was walking down Clark Street towards her apartment, she heard a scuffle. She turned around and saw the guys with the back packs encircling the old woman with the Aldi bags.

This was her shining moment.

"What the fuck are you doing?" She screamed as she heaved her chubby intoxicated body towards the men.

"Leave her alone." She jumped on the shorter of the two grabbing him around the neck just as two cop cars pulled up.

The old lady started crying. "This crazy bitch was attacking these sweet boys who were going to help carry groceries to my apartment."

Meghan put her hand to her mouth. One of the cops took her name and phone number. Instead of apologizing she too started crying.

She was sober by the time she entered her apartment. Before she took off her coat she cleaned the litter box and took the garbage downstairs to the alley. She removed the many posters in her living room of Tina Fey and other Second City alumni. She put on her flannel men's pajama bottoms decorated in reindeer and a Second City sweatshirt and begin to clean. She got on her hands and knees and washed the floors. She scrubbed the bathroom and kitchen with bleach. She cleared food cartons and receipts off the top of her grandmother's mahogany buffet and polished it. When she finally lay down on fresh sheets she felt as unsullied as she did as a child in her princess themed bedroom in Council Bluffs, Iowa.

The next morning, she was drinking coffee and muddling over a litany of her embarrassing moments when the doorbell rang." Hi Meghan, I'm John Merrill from

WGN news. We understand you tried to apprehend some young men last night."

She pulled at her bangs and giggled."Yep. That's me. The town idiot."

"Oh, no not at all. In fact, we'd like to feature last night's incident on the five o'clock news. It's a great story. Not many people are willing to get involved with helping others in distress."

"Jesus Mary and Joseph!" She muttered . Did she hear this right?

She had the day off and at ten o'clock took a bus to Marshalls, a department store that advertises "Your surprise is waiting." She ascended the escalator feeling as if she was going up to heaven. She bought a green cashmere sweater and black pants and at two o'clock she was applying her new MAC makeup. It was more than she expected. Cameras were set up and several unidentified people were standing around looking officious. Meghan wasn't nervous. In fact, she was ebullient. The interview took a mere ten minutes, but the crew was there for over an hour. People were standing around downstairs in front of the shoe store certain there had been a murder.

She called her family in Iowa. Her mother started weeping.

"Oh, my god. To think I ever underestimated my pumpkin."

It was all that she had dreamed of when she was drinking Manhattans in Logan Square. But now she was exhausted. "Too much" she kept repeating.

The first call the following morning was from the Shirley Hamilton Talent Agency "Hi Meghan, my name is Audrey and I'd like to take you on as a client."

She took extra minutes to curl her hair and arrived at work ten minutes early. Kate was at her computer and never mentioned Meghan's new celebrity.

"Hey Meg. Buy us some coffee."

Meghan was glowing like the shop windows in the morning. She bought two large coffees and a croissant for Kate and wouldn't take her money. She cheerfully straightened the clothes and chatted with the customers. She had an unexpected longing for her home in Council Bluffs. She had left to escape what she called the' Council Bluffs curse'. She remembered those state fairs and those sickly-looking families, emaciated young fathers walking slightly ahead looking both bewildered and belligerent and the teen mothers with a baby clinging to their halter top. Meghan couldn't abide the bow-legged farmers in dirty overalls and offhanded gaiety as they perused their future slaughter. Vegans were called "Snowflakes" and Chicago was a godless hell hole of "illegals." Megan knew her dreams, albeit still vague, would have eventually dissolved into her mother's souf-flé. After a few weeks, she would go back to recognizing Al and Beth Yoder as royalty because they owned Trust Insurance and within a year, she would succumb to a Pampered Chef party. Just the thought of it made her whimper. Her mother had sent a picture of her prom date,Ryan Anderson writing that he was still single ,a firefighter and member of the city council. He hadn't changed much but she had. She recognized the intractable smugness of stupidity. His flushed chubby cheeks, flaccid chin and beady eyes reminded her of an unbaked cookie. But she stopped at Pet Smart on the way home and purchased a cat carrier just in case. She stopped at Hop Leaf on Clark and ordered a beer at the bar. A friend from Second City called her over to a table. Brian introduced her to his new roommate, Rich, who had just moved to Chicago.

"It's Wonder Woman."

She recognized him immediately as one of the guys on the bus."Oh god. I'm sorry. I just got carried away. I watch too many crime shows."

"I thought it was very cool. You're very chivalrous."

"We were going to go back to my apartment. Come back with us."

Brian's courtyard apartment building was a block from Meghan's. It encircled a garden with a bronze statue of a milk maiden. The residents look like people who go to neighborhood block parties and write to their congressman. They make day long trips to Ikea and have photos of their travels along a hallway. Brian was like that. He dabbled in theater but majored in economics at Loyola.

A warm and brilliant sun took its evening leave by splashing its rays on a small red and white rug. Meghan was enveloped in its warmth. The voices became a serenade. She watched the lovely lips move up and down as Rich talked about law school and his large family back in Sioux City, Iowa. She refused a second beer because she was falling asleep. On the second landing she heard her name.

"Meghan, I'd like to see you again." He had beseeching blue eyes and how would she explain that he was bold and shy at the same time.

Years later when she's asked, she can't remember exactly the first time she knew she was in love, but she tells her children it was on that landing.

Chapter 4

Now I Lay Me

Mary is in bed studying a scummy heating vent and twenty-three year old trim while trying to visualize the bedroom after it is painted. She is listening to Mike rustling in the kitchen and wondering when this attractive easy going man had become a saver of paper plates. She has known Mike most of her adult life because thirty some years ago she had been married to his brother Owen. That previous winter the building's manager had discovered Owen's nicotine wracked body during a routine morning wellness check. Mike paid for his brother's memorial and two weeks following the burial at Ascension Cemetery he asked her out. At one time Mike would not necessarily have been her type because she had been drawn to anguished souls who adhered their emaciated haunches to her couch and looked at her in adulation while drinking boxed wine and quoting Kahlil Gibran. Mike on the other hand had a sure footed nonchalance that would have portended heartache for a high strung girl like herself. Both before and after his first marriage she remembers him at those numerous family barbecues always with some woman sitting on an adjacent plastic webbed beach chair with an imploring expression ; a voluptuous gabby debutant named Vicki Flaherty followed by a few sullen beauties with inscrutable expressions.

She feels extraordinarily fortunate to love someone with the ardor with which she loves Mike. Alone in the guest room she tries to recall being in love with Owen at twenty two. She had met him one Friday night at a Chicago bar called Butch Maguire's.He had reminded her of John F. Kennedy with a touch of F Scott Fitzgerald and she clung to that mirage until one too many calls from General Finance broke the spell.

With Mike she had once again lost her footing with that first kiss. All those years of dissecting the subject of love with furrowed brow and somber friends it was, alas, that kiss that changed everything just as it had fifty some years ago. And from a sirocco of panting and pressing and smoking weed they had settled into a schedule of Mass on Saturday evenings followed by a trip to the grocery store and dinner at his place in Kenosha, Wisconsin.

He had given her a ring at Christmas. At first she had insisted he sell his condo and they live in Chicago but he persuaded her that redoing his place was a smarter idea and when she imagined herself and her daughter, Eileen shopping at Home Goods and perusing furniture stores she acquiesced. To Mary, Mike has maintained a sexiness that even his twenty year old plaid Van Heusen shirts could not diminish. And in spite of the fact that he saves florid greeting cards sent to him from numerous Catholic charities he still reminds her of Mark Harmon. And even though he has five years of cancelled checks he inspires her to read love quotes and purchase bikini underpants and a sixty dollar lip plumper at Nordstrom's. By now all of this is moot. He is an exorable presence. She is a domesticated feral ; A world in which she once roamed undaunted would now seem perilous without him. Yet on this morning within the fading paint and shredding lilac trim Mary ponders the future. She is hungover from last night's martinis and he is making oatmeal that has the color of dead skin. She still won't see him without makeup and wonders if he realizes that. She especially needs something called Liquid Roses which she applies to her cheeks before she leaves the bedroom. He doesn't know that her underwear used to be cotton Hanes and her new seventy dollar bras are only for him while the puny padded things are clumped in the third drawer of her dresser in the Chicago apartment she shares with Eileen and her granddaughter, Lily.

Mike has suggested they go to Menards to look at paint shades. It is snowing with the wanton impudence of Wisconsin snow. The streets are intractable requiring cautious driving and rumination. She is thinking about whether or not they should replace carpeting with flooring while he is lamenting over gas prices. Mary is wearing a casual outfit which was not casual in its forethought, a pair of new work out pants in a muted leopard print and a sixty dollar velour jacket. Instead of the places she had once fantasized for these clothes she was thrust into a store of glaring lights and complicated looking gadgets. She remembered a song about 'Dear hearts and gentle people who live and love in my home town.' Were these people with tattoos and behemoth bodies gentle? Or dear? Mike is absorbed in an animated conversation about a step ladder.

"Hey Herb, this is my fiancée, Mary. We're kind of setting up shop so to speak. You know, new furniture etc.. "

"So what do you think about this stepladder, Honey? It's like a feather to carry and it extends. " She considered saying "That's what he said" but resisted.

The idea that he ever reminded her of James Dean is becoming more outlandish by the minute. And now he is swooning over a lantern.

They purchase the stepladder and an overhead reading lamp which Mike gloated over as if he had discovered electricity.

"I just got a text from Kevin. I think we should have him over tonight for dinner. Maybe salmon and baked potato, simple stuff and you can toss together one of your spectacular salads."

Mary adores Mikes' son, Kevin and is wondering what spectacular salad he is referring to while they drive to Walmart. She is remembering something in the Bible about cleaving to one's spouse and going to Walmart in Racine requires serious cleaving because she struts and Mike ambles and she often loses track of him. The store lacks the visual appeal of HomeGoods, a place that gorges on cute and where she is given to fondling dish towels with daisies and soap dispensers in the shape of frogs. Walmart is an " in and out" kind of store. But she does pick up a five dollar t-shirt with a cat on it. Something she will only wear to Walmart. She locates Mike in hardware, a man on a mission. They decide on a cake for dessert. The weather is vicious. But no Dr Zhivago. Instead there is a grimacing man squinting at the windshield and a woman with a cat t- shirt in her purse looking flummoxed.

When Kevin has left and her makeup is removed she once again takes stock of the guest bedroom where she now sleeps and hangs her clothing. There is no tv. He is impressed with her prodigious reading and recent attempts at painting and doesn't yet realize that she is slavishly addicted to Bravo and instead of stunning mankind with her creativity she occasionally prefers to lie in bed and gape at women fighting in restaurants.

The following morning she makes her bed and packs. It should be a simple chore but there is always a misplaced item. Today she is looking under the sheets for Emerson, one of the books she has been forcing upon herself as a part of her new bucolic life. She has briefly entertained giving up Tito's but only briefly. The drive back is always more monotonous then the train ride there when she fantasizes she is in a film with subtitles.

In spite of a life that has often proven otherwise she has persisted in believing she is dancing down a street called Happiness in a technicolor musical. And by the following Friday she can only remember the crinkles when he smiles and the way he dances to Beautiful by Heart in his boxers. And once again she is aflutter in another new dress, this one is decorated in dachshunds and swings when she walks looking like who she is, one incapable of a hard bargain. Unfortunately his bathroom mirror is clearer than hers and last weekend she discovered more wrinkles which called for another trip to Macys where a chatty lady sold her eighty dollar serum from an "Australian rich yeast ferment complex". And all this for four o'clock mass with windbag Father Coughlan. That night she googled 'living room couches' and fretted over her beloved cats Ace and Trixie. Would Mike understand Trixie's mysterious emotional traumas that result in pee droplets? And Ace is a climber.

As she is packing her phone rings. It is her niece, Betsy who lives in Tampa. Her sister, Liz has died. Mary is both stunned and mystified. Not that she wasn't old but she wasn't the dying type. She was twelve years older and remained to Mary a flawless aloof beauty. She was a wit and an intellect and it occurred to her that morning that she had never dated a man, read a book or had an idea that she didn't look to Liz for approval and now she had abandoned her. Here she was, a seventy old woman feeling like a lost kid as she listened to details about Liz's recent illness. The idea of strangers coming the next day to remove her bed and clothing. was appalling. Her sister, so private and persnickety dying in Depends was like desecrating the tabernacle. She sobbed like a child all night and only briefly considered it somehow sacrilegious to return to Kenosha the next day.

In keeping with her abiding sense of drama taking the Metra train affords a brief moment of intrigue when she texts Mike to tell him which car she is on. She often sees him first and sees a beautiful man neither young or old. She sees the beseeching blue eyes, the half-smile, the feet turned slightly outward and sees both continual discovery along with sublime familiarity; a man who carefully reads her writing and accepts her frailties. She takes note of the way he holds his right hand on his thigh when driving; a subtle reminder of belligerent days. And for a moment she wishes him just that, to be eighteen again in his Camaro taking happiness for granted with Vicki Flaherty's tits at his disposal.

They decide on October sixteenth for no specific reason. Mary isn't detail oriented and in fact the mere mention of the word 'form' gives her the heebie jeebies. But a wedding requires details and one morning she enters a place called Love Notes in Chicago where women wear Lululemon workout clothing on their concave bodies and have long-suffering expressions. To her inquiry about wedding invitations the salesperson replies "Oh that's so cute" and "We now do it online". Mary thanks her and sniffs some heart shaped candles on the way out. Mike suggests they look into places near Kenosha. They find a family owned printing business in a town called Caledonia that could be reached through winding oddly named roads past farms and homes barely visible behind trees and deer statuary. She imagined they were in a Hallmark movie until they could no longer see addresses and Mike was muttering obscenities.

In spite of a gradual move each weekend the actual move is traumatic. Mary is embarking on a colossal adventure, without a daughter, granddaughter or subway train and Eileen has become exceptionally perky over the idea of transforming her bedroom into an office.

At the beginning of May they order furniture and in June the painter arrives. Except for the invitations and disc Jockey wedding plans are not as seamless as she had imagined they would be. Caterers were not calling back and the priest required a dossier equivalent to joining the CIA and a day of waiting in lines in downtown Chicago. Gradually she is becoming a quivering sycophant trying to navigate a strange world driven by etiquette and expedience in a universe where prices have no relevance. In a more lucid state she would have thought it bizarre to pay five hundred dollars for a few bouquets, two altar vases and two boutonnières.

The last two weeks are more convivial and those she had accused of being dismissive rally at the end. On the evening before her wedding her family throws a shower in her hotel room replete with sassy underwear and champagne. The following morning her daughter and granddaughter do her hair and makeup. The three women drive the few miles over to the chapel where they wait in a sunny room while the photographer takes too many pictures. From where she stands she can see the guests arrive. At five till one a lady by the name of Sheila takes them to a small enclosure by the sanctuary and she and Eileen wait for the longest five minutes of her life.

And then her eldest son Brendan is by her side and Mike is at the alter looking beautiful in his new suit. Sheila beckons the flower girl, then Eileen and then Mary. And for that brief moment in time she sees beyond her beloved Mike into that unsullied kingdom of her childhood when she had claimed this moment.

Chapter 5

Gracie's Wing

She had moved to Willow Grove, Wisconsin the previous summer and married Terry the following October, a ceremony befitting the remarkable betrothal of Anne and Terry O'Malley. Or as her daughter had remarked more than once something she couldn't "wrap her head around" and indeed even Anne who is given to frequent flights of fancy could never have imagined.

Anne had been living a pleasant but somewhat rag tag existence. She had the back bedroom of a Chicago apartment shared with her daughter and granddaughter and the reassuring routine of museums and used book stores. In other words there was no lead up to this spectacular turn of events.

Anne had been divorced over twenty years from Patrick O'Malley when she received a call from his building manager one winter morning as she was preparing for a dental appointment. They had discovered his body during their morning wellness check. Instead of a filling Anne found herself staring at the man who had once reminded her of John Kennedy now lying perpendicular on his twin bed as if he'd made one last stab at life.

Patrick's brother, Terry paid for the memorial and in the Spring he asked her to dinner. It was a simple courtship but for Anne it was the culmination of everything she had not known she'd wanted. He would pick her up on Saturday afternoon and they would attend four o'clock Mass in Willow Grove followed by a stop at the grocers and dinner. Unassuming fare to most but to Anne it entailed a drastic weight loss, eighty dollar bras and in place of her cotton Hanes, frilly uncomfortable crotch crawling lace panties.

Enmeshed in romantic thoughts and a size two wardrobe Anne hadn't confronted the vast contrast between Chicago and Willow Grove. This came as no surprise to her kids who have always speculated over their mother's astounding capacity for exuberance; an uncanny ability to transform the ordinary into a fifties musical. She made a seamless transition from book stores to Hobby Lobby and wreath making and in January she volunteered for a Sunday afternoon at the Willow Grove Art Center. Unbeknownst to Terry she expended hours of thought over her impending role as greeter. She had her hair touched up and purchased a thirty dollar contour stick that promised a more chiseled face.

That Sunday morning as she watched a tutorial on the application of her contour stick she was imagining today as a life changing pursuit, a moment she would relate at a future awards luncheon. Willow Grove's future docent darling was in a dither as she entered the art center with the expectancy of visiting royalty. She was met by three flummoxed expressions. Was she in the right place? Was her contour stick smeared?

"Hi! I'm here to be a greeter this afternoon."

The responses remained steadfastly abstruse; disdain or the affixed expressions of dullards. She couldn't be sure. But she was sure that there would be no name tag or sign in sheet, just two arthritic women and one middle aged cripple who introduced himself as Jeff.

"Hi. What brings you her?" Jeff asked in the tremulous voice of a plane crash survivor.

Still in her cocktail party mode Anne attempted to regale Jeff with her tale of late life romance. In turn Jeff told her how he had met his girlfriend of ten years at a comic book convention.

The other two were hobbling throughout the first floor, one whose name was Arlene alighted on a stool in the gift shop with her newspaper.

"Have you been volunteering here long?" Anne inquired of Jeff.

"Yes." he whispered with the same desperate expression.

"Fucking god. Now what?" She was calculating the tedium of the next two hours and forty five minutes when the most formidable looking of the three came back to the desk.

"How's your mother, Jeffrey. I don't see you two at Mass anymore?"

A scene from Tennessee Williams flashed before her.

Anne never caught her name but it began with "M" and wasn't soft and reassuring like Mary or Molly but short and pugnacious like its owner."M" had a nasally voice and a mystifyingly short puffy bob resembling a helmet, brutal looking jaws and the nonexistent lips of a die hard party pooper.

"Someone just called and wants to buy that brass fish upstairs. I'm not sure how to work that credit card gismo." "M" said as she was furiously scratching her helmet.

"Why don't I go upstairs and put a sold sticker on the fish?" Anne was still feeling somewhat sassy with her newly contoured face.

"M" gave her a sticker and as Anne hunted for the fish she pretended she was curating new pieces at Chicago's Art Institute. Her daydream was short lived because the second floor was divided into separate alcoves with several aquatic pieces.

She was panicky."Could I be fired from a volunteer job?"

Ten minutes later she triumphantly descended the staircase feeling like a silver screen actress.

"I found the fish."

"M" and Jeffery stared at her as if she were a stranger.

A few couples breezed in and out eschewing the mailing list. A group of decrepit looking people emerged from a mini bus withy Sassy Seniors painted on its side. Clinging to one another like drunkards they headed towards the gift shop and Arlene. Anne was becoming antsy. If she remained at the desk she would be fodder for "M" who had frowned upon hearing that she was a newlywed from Chicago.

"Perhaps I should see what's going on upstairs." she offered.

"Gracie does the upstairs wing," said "M" with a force that caused Anne to grab the corner of the desk. The mouth didn't close it clamped. The helmet seemed to levitate. Where was Gracie when was searching for the fish? It was all too much and she needed a break.

When Anne returned from the washroom Gracie, a tiny apparition in black resembling a startled crow, Arlene, "M" and a woman to whom she was not introduced were discussing Ash Wednesday Masses and M's doll collection. Anne slipped in a bon mot about her addiction to book stores to which "M" replied, "Those dirty places wreak havoc on my deviated spectrum."

The women glared at her and continued discussing M's latest acquisition, Princess Dianna from eBay for a mere two hundred dollars.

She expected a consolation gift for an afternoon with savages when she fell into the car. But Terry was nonchalantly debating pizza or pasta for dinner. Anne tried to explain the phantom from the upstairs wing and the less than gracious greeters.

Here was a man whom she so loved that he was able to wrest from her the sublime life of a feral city dweller who found joy not in nature but in urban vibrance. She was suddenly grief stricken.

But the lake was positively shimmering like something she'd seen only in a childhood book. She took his small boulder of a hand remembering miracles that only she knew; a reprieve from mortality, a redemption from her chronic unrest and a glimpse into the Divine.

"Pizza sounds great."

Chapter 6

My Teeth and Dr. Levin

We all have teeth or at least we have had them at one time. They are not a source of interest, let alone literature. Thirty-two little white things made of enamel. If anything, they are a source of jokes, those annoying little guys in the attic with nicknames like choppers and clappers like perpetual kids, always up to some shenanigans. chomp chomp.

My earliest memory of dentistry is of my mom and I debarking the Howard Street bus at what was called the bus barn at Howard and Clark in Chicago. From there we proceeded down Howard, she in no nonsense pumps, a housedress with a handkerchief and chicklets in its cavernous pocket, me, chronically anemic, constipated, and nervous. If it wasn't the dentist, it was the atom bomb. The building was an inner sanctum of dank smelling dark corridors and a wobbly elevator. Dr Dubrow had a receding hairline, tiny mustache, and a drill that he unraveled. With his marshmallow-like hand and fingers dotted in tiny black hairs he placed it upon my teeth, thirty-two burgeoning miscreants, scheming right there literally under my nose.

Nothing is hotter than Federal Highway at three in the afternoon in Hollywood, Florida where we lived during my eighth grade. But every week I made the steamy pilgrimage from St Theresa's to Dr Duda's until twelve cavities were filled. My only distraction was thinking about Gary Dones, the relentless bane of Sister Andrew Irene. It would not be a good day if Gary wasn't in trouble; my beautiful crusty, dusky swaggering Gary. Even the name, so blatantly pagen, thrilled me. I looked innocent enough, like my St Cecelia holy card, with my white complexion, high forehead and small pensive mouth but I had scathing thoughts regarding Gary and me. Sore and sweaty I would make the return trip down Federal Highway to our yellow stucco house and lay under a window fan until dinner.

I'm not going to plague the reader with a detailed anatomy of my teeth work. But they don't work in consort with the rest of me. I can enter a dentist's office feeling robust and learn that one of those stinkers residing in the "mesial" part of my mouth needs instant attention and unlike other clinical procedures there's no actual finite fix. They abide in my mouth rotating like a Rube Goldberg device.; One filling, two filling, three filling, pull. And back again.

I can't attribute genes to every problem of those errant squatters. I'm certain that part of my oral tribulation is due to long spells of neglect when I was single and living in various cavernous apartments in Chicago and spending my money on boxed wine and Brides Magazines. But after I married I returned to the biannual checkups and it was during that period that a dentist had to stop in the middle of an extraction and send me to a specialist fifteen miles away.

After I was divorced my children and I moved a mile West of my childhood home off Devon Avenue on the Northside of Chicago. Devon never changes. The pigeons poop with the unabashed abandon of creatures who have come from a long line of Devon poopers. And once again I was searching for a dentist.Not more than a mile from our apartment and only slightly brighter than the foreboding halls of Dr Debrow's was the office of young Dr Levin, He shared his practice with an elderly dentist (he was probably younger than I am today) Dr Moses who told Yiddish jokes while his liver spotted hands worked with deft tenderness. I went to both depending on my schedule until Dr Moses retired to Ft Meyers, Fl and then it was me and Dr Levin. I remember pictures of his young boys in soccer outfits that sat on his counter and served as a distraction. By now drills were mercifully quick and Doctor Levin offered nitrous in a pinch. His young and cheerful hygienist,Delia doubled as his receptionist. Although chronically short on cash while working for the city of Winnetka, I was flush with benefits. Dr Levin recommended a costly and somewhat uncomfortable treatment called scaling, a prophylactic against future periodontal problems.

Dr levin eventually proceeded westward to the tony neighborhood of Sauganash and I followed with my dental woes. The photos in his office had gone from soccer to cap and gowns. Having fallen prey to chardonnay and usury credit card interest I was both plump and litigious. Mastercard might have been hounding me but at least I had my dental insurance and Dr Levin.

My daughter had a baby. I quit the Winnetka library to watch Lily. Dr levin moved again. He hired an hygienist, Maureen. I had no insurance, but my teeth did not care. Delia's daughter was in high school. Dr Levin's mother died; a son married. My daughter and I, for reasons so fanciful I wish not to expound upon, moved to Southeast Florida. It was hot. My teeth would play games with me, little stabs then nothing. I had no insurance. The dental office near our complex, Hiatus featured a smiling cuspid with a toothbrush in his hand. It signified everything I hated about the place.

We moved back. Two teeth were beyond saving, Dr Levin's other son got married, the other produced a film. Delia's daughter went away to college.

I had to go to Dr Levin the day following the death of my son. This time it was a phantom tooth. An ache no doubt from something else. For once my teeth had the decorum to step aside. Delia and Maureen went to the funeral.

Lily became an adult. Maureen's house caught on fire, Delia got married, separated and remarried. I fell in love. My front tooth had the impunity to break a week before my wedding. After he bonded it, Dr Levin warned me that it was a temporary fix.

The following Spring during a routine cleaning he announced he and his wife were going to see the tulips in Amsterdam. Not having him in the country for two weeks was disquieting. My teeth and I were on edge during his absence living on smoothies and cottage cheese while he photographed flowers.

In June I was enduring an agonizingly long procedure, the final indignation of partial dentures when he announced he was retiring.

Today we said goodbye. And tonight, my decrepit incisors, corroded molars, new partials, scaled gums and I are bereft. Dr Levin and I were never able to remedy my unfortunate set of teeth. But we floated through many chapters together and I must admit each one ended pretty well.

Chapter 7

My child

You do know. Don't you?
That the dead aren't always dying.

My son was once sprinting by the lake
brooding over money
and women
and things I never understood.

His silence was sacred.
The protruding chin
The long fingers tapping the sweaty blond hair
while pondering what?
Sex?
Kierkegaard?
Who knows?
Who ever knows
the back alleys

of another's soul?

If I'd only known that he would die
(And so did I... almost)
If I'd only known those alabaster shoulder blades
were fleeting
That a cherub's cry at night was music
The house in which we dwelt was not a chore but
Heaven....And only then in the midst of fury had I
glimpsed at God.
How was I to know that the wrath and the worry
and the Lysol
was a subterfuge?
How would I have known that at that kitchen table
with its nonsensical talk and
mismatched dishes
that my child
would unabashedly leave this earth.

I wished away my days...not knowing
those wisps of humanity were my Graces
.... my Elysium
And now scents and songs accosts me
like Stations of the Cross.

Chapter 8

Adios

At one time the word "vacation" harkened back to those mesmerizing and infinite hours of counting telephone poles and feeling exquisitely errant eating cold cereal and a powdered doughnut in some funky little motor court. These sweet memories, clouded with time, were replaced by the glamour of flight and any trepidation over the viability of aeronautics was quelled by a cigarette and a drink. But 9/11 removed whatever remnant of romance remained of air travel. Trepidation over a possible plane crash was overshadowed by the idea of a terrorist lurking at my gate. Signs reading "If you see something, say something" took the fun out of cocktails. And for reasons I can't fully explain there was a period of at least five years when I did not fly.

I watched shows on PBS that made car trips look like fun; travelers stopping along the way to chat with the locals while picking up handmade bracelets and straw hats. Even the family dog is included in these heart-warming shenanigans. My daughter and granddaughter and I giddily set out at dawn one March headed for Southeast Florida and my sister.

By the time we beheld "Welcome to Florida" with an orange in place of the 'O' I was teary eyed. The Florida turnpike was an endless terrain of nothing. Even the palm trees saved themselves for later. Those diners I loved when I was five became my idea of Purgatory. Were the menus always that big and dirty? And were people always that fat? Engorged pedal pushers and a sea of half-baked lifeless faces would not have inspired Whitman's "I Sing the Body Electric." I beheld a three generational herd of behemoth, splay legged bipeds at a service plaza in Port St. Lucie. A flat headed boy who could have been a large thirteen year old slapped a barrel chested female who looked like someone out of a Diane Arbus collection. She had not more than twenty purple strands of hair snaking down her doughy neck and purple tattoos dribbling down the back of her calves. I took her to be the mother until what looked like a water rat in a halter top intervened and knocked the kid across the head. By the time we hit Hibiscus Hamlet in Plantation. Florida my left calf was numb and any sliver of agape was over-shadowed by an unbridled, atavistic yearning for normal food. We stayed four days which hardly compensated for the two day trip.

Of all the paltry things over which I would fret in those occult pre-dawn hours two events occurred that I couldn't have imagined. My youngest son died and the following year the world was torn asunder by a deadly virus that paralyzed all form of travel. Somehow, and this is why I'm still a believer in an unknown benevolent Force, out of grief and uncertainty came love. I got married.

My husband Terry, being the even keeled amiable American that he is, anticipates travel with the ingenuous zeal of a kid taking an eighth grade field trip. If he's got a backpack with clean underwear and a change of clothes he's at one with the world. The good news about love in later life is that it's the same. The bad news; it's the same. I'm just as blinded. Love casts a blazing pastel hue over everything. Visiting a cousin became a Doris Day musical as I envisioned our trip to Delray Beach, Florida. I pictured our bodies, transformed into lithe and youthful limbs, cavorting on a king size bed emitting the wanton scent of beach and suntan oil. At dawn his cousin, Sheila was skittering around like an escaped gerbil. And precisely at seven minutes to seven she was softly knocking on our door so Terry could accompany her to Mass. For some reason I would have preferred a hell and damnation banging to her deference. There was an implicit message that I, Anne O'Malley am a hedonist who drinks martinis while preferring earthly pleasures to the hereafter. She had purchased three snorkels and envisioned the three of us snorkeling in her pool. I declined and chose to separate myself as the cousins romped in the water like arthritic Bobbsey Twins.

A year later and Terry has that glint in his eye. It's that one time when he abandons his roster of money saving tricks like reusing paper plates and almost throws caution to the wind. Almost. His cousin was not in Florida this year but my niece, Betty had extended an invitation to her "villa." A small house is not called a small house in her community but a villa, a vernacular compatible with Disney World a mile down highway 4. I lived in Hollywood, Florida for eight years as a kid moving from Chicago for my father's failing health. And in all those years I never heard the names of the towns in which Betty has lived. Her latest is Champion Gate which was preceded by Celebration. They aren't towns as in the reassuring little places portrayed in movies where boys walk down a country road with fishing rods and women put apple pies between their kitchen shears to cool. These are assemblages of stucco "villas" interspersed with pools, golf courses and smug faces waving from their golf carts.

In an attempt to show off his tech prowess Terry took a screen shot of the rental car confirmation for Orlando. And, bless his heart he purchased tickets through something called Cheap Air. Imagine if you will these two details followed by Toccata and Fugue in D minor on the organ. In my usual fanciful manner I was more caught up in new shorts and daydreams than practicality. The Spirit trip went smoothly enough but an hour away from Orlando an unsettling thought overshadowed my excitement. Upon looking at the photo of the rent-a -car receipt I realized the actual company name had not been included. Terry reassured me that the words "Economy" next to the amount meant Economy Rental. In order to reach Economy Rental we first had to wait for a shuttle bus in Mesozoic kind of heat then proceed down by-ways and highway, our asses lurching to and fro on the tweed seats. Only one person was allowed in the tiny rental office so I gladly sat in a waiting room with a coke until a slightly distorted, perspiring face appeared at the adjoining window. It was Terry. The confirmation number did not match theirs. I took one more swig of my diet cola and regained some equilibrium. The resolution was in Terry's hands as the long suffering agent explained. Terry would have received a follow up email since it was on his credit card. But alas! Terry's phone had been teetering on death for weeks barely able to manage simple duties, one being email. Under the gentle caresses of Marci and her violet fingernails she was finally able to retrieve his information and determine it was Ace Rental. I had reached an out of body state fueled by anxiety, heat and annoyance and was deliriously composing letters to the head of Economy with praise for Marci. We had to hitch a ride on Economy's shuttle back to the airport to wait for another shuttle to take us to Ace Rent a Car. Perhaps Eric, the driver, sensed an upcoming conniption fit because he drove us directly to Ace.

My niece Betty lives in a place created by Disney. It's. a. place. But the GPS lady begged to differ as to its existence. My teeth were starting their usual nonsense. They tend to gang up on me when I'm in the throes of a real or imagined crisis. For instance when my sister died my tooth fell out while I was crying. My ex-husband's death was overshadowed by a raunchy molar that needed an immediate root canal. Two weeks before my wedding another broken molar got all sensitive on me over a simple cracker which necessitated a Sunday emergency room visit. After Betty explained that the "place" also goes by the name of Davenport we got on Interstate 4 along with a blur of cars slouching their way to Happiness. Instead of turning off at Disney World we entered Champion Gate with its pompous curlicue letters and a sweaty security guard dressed like the Royal Bahamas police. My tooth rallied with the help of a martini and air conditioning.

The following day Terry and I took off for a sentimental journey to Hollywood. We decided to take the scenic route instead of the tollway . It started pleasantly enough in the vein of those endearing PBS documentaries; getting all folksy with proprietors of thrift stores along the way. By Vero Beach I'd had enough of that hokey nonsense. And God Almighty, it was turning into a long damn trip. By the time we found our place nestled between other buttery stucco huts along the boardwalk I had forgotten why this was such a good idea. The manager of The Hacienda advised us to get out of the nearby parking lot immediately or risk a tow. In exchange for twenty dollars Terry was given a sticker for his windshield and proceeded to look for a legal spot. After circling A1A for twenty minutes he located one six blocks away. I had envisioned something entirely different while in our Wisconsin condo. Squealing with excitement we would throw our backpacks on the bed and hand in hand we would skip down to the ocean. There we would romp in the water until we were slightly chilled and afterwards we would succumb to our repressed Midwestern sexual fantasies followed by a dinner at a tiki bar. My astonishing sense of romance is both a charm and a curse. By the time he came weaving up the sidewalk Terry was too tired to go out. He fetched some odd overpriced Mexican concoction on the boardwalk that we ate in our room. The next morning we did a short walk at dawn and collected a few seashells. I showed him my old house and we stopped at a diner on Federal Highway where I'd eaten as a kid. The food was served suspiciously fast and only slightly warmed. Terry did not want the turnpike which had something to do with the rental car and fees. Despite directing our GPS otherwise that bitch of a voice kept trying to commandeer us back to the turnpike which necessitated rerouting and U-turns and gnashing of the teeth. I was deliriously happy to see the curlicues.

The following day Betty and I shopped while Terry used the putting green. We had a lovely farewell dinner and left the next morning two hours before our flight in order to return the car. Our gate was in a section in what I now refer to as the "buffoon encampment." I bought some candy and water and we proceeded to look at our phones and people. Thinking I heard our airline's name (they all had goofy names) and "delay" I walked through strollers and wheelchairs and over supine bodies to look at the monitor. Dear god. I thought I was hallucinating. How could a plane be delayed by three hours? The other funky planes were delayed as well judging from the amount of stagnating humanity. Up to this point and in spite of having four children I had somehow managed to avoid Disneyworld and here it was in all its cranky bilious residue. Every few minutes someone would let out a loud moan which on my third trip to the commissary I traced to a wheelchair. By the time we settled at our gate Terry was catatonic. For some reason the relief of imminent boarding had the opposite effect on me. The woman next to me happened to be from the same small town in Wisconsin as my daughter-in-law and suddenly she, with her frazzled nest of hair and darting eyes (she was popping pills "for her back") was my new best friend. Our seats 32 a and b were surrounded by children and parents who believed in gentle reasoning. For some reason it took forty minute to lodge the luggage in cargo. There was no air and one rambunctious little shit kept kicking my seat. I was on the verge of a panic attack when reason overtook me. If I caused a delay in takeoff I might be stoned by my fellow passengers.

Milwaukee in all its frigid gray looked fabulous. The cats were glad to see us especially the male who has the personality of a Golden Retriever. I realized something while doing our laundry the following week. The heavens are good to Terry. Maybe it's those daily Masses.

He might leave out travel information but a man whose socks always come back in pairs abides with the angels.

Chapter 9

The Kennedy Boy

Nothing was easy about going out in damp forty degree weather. Nancy had lived in Chicago most of her life but the first cold day was fraught with discussion and deliberation. People talked about the coming winter as if a missile crisis was looming on the horizon. Her ex-husband John was in the hospital. That previous Monday he had trouble breathing in the checkout line of Jewel Foods and the manager had called the paramedics. Before getting dressed Nancy had coffee and her smorgasbord of whatever newest potions promised eternal youth including a packet of turmeric, honey and kale dissolved in water. She didn't believe any of it but like her Novenas at St Clem's Church she wasn't taking any chances.

"He would pick this kind of weather to get sick," she had said when her daughter, Mary notified her. He was never, even at his testosterone prime, a hearty, sanguine sort of fellow. Before she left him she had concluded that he was happy being unhappy and her marriage was starting to read like one of those tragic Irish memoirs. But at twenty-two when she met him at a bar on Division street in Chicago she had been in love or something akin to a frenzy over this bleating lamb who looked like John F. Kennedy and whose silent tantrums she mistook for creative brooding. But the toothy mouth never cracked a poem. After their divorce a relationship of necessity and affection slowly weaved its way through holidays, grandchildren and loneliness. Nancy always hoped for a sliver of levity during their lunch dates. But something always went awry like poppyseed getting stuck in his teeth prompting the long milky fingers to flutter and spittle to fly. This latest emergency has a perverse celebratory aspect to it. Her son Frank is coming in from Milwaukee.

Mary was waiting for her in the hospital's lobby "Another fucking medical crisis and I've got a million emails to answer. He should have quit smoking a million years ago."

"He didn't and right now I'm trying to remember that recipe for pasta and mushrooms that Frank was so crazy about the last time he was here. Did I use spinach? Yes. I think I did."

The hospital with its artificial light and flowers filled Nancy with terror. Someone was playing a Frank Sinatra tune on the piano. Looking at a plate of lifeless cookies was like looking down the tunnel of death: A cruel joke to play on a couple who got their soft unblemished hands stamped at Butch McGuires. They were a snotty pair; Nancy with her Sassoon haircut ,smidgeon of regal lips and wondrously blue eyes; John in his Lacoste shirt and prep school cockiness. He and his friends would meet on Friday nights to discuss their vague future and flirt; the nape of their necks slightly damp and smelling of English Leather. Now people saw John as a stooped old man roaming the aisles of Jewel Foods..

The hospital's visitors were mostly old and gabby, no doubt grateful to have once again escaped the gauntlet. The women especially frightened her. They reminded her of the ones at bus stops who seemed to be slowly decomposing like spring worms. John's room was down a myriad of corridors with spokes that led to the nurses' station. John was watching Family Feud or rather it was on and his face was tilted in that direction. A curtain divided him and another patient but she could hear the soft and labored snoring. A burly aide came in.

"Hey there, John. Let's get a little blood from ya. Show me those muscles."

He was talking in the off handed chatty manner of a fitness coach. Nancy wished hospitals had retained their old decorum when nurses in crisp uniforms somberly tended to the sick. Those were the days when one knew where they stood.

Nancy want downstairs for coffee and called her sister, Maggie in Delray Beach, Florida."This is getting hard for me to take. And he could have prevented it."

"We all have our thing, Nancy. Some spend, some drink, and some eat themselves silly. You are his family. I told you years ago to try Parents Without Partners but you thought love would appear in the produce aisle."

"I met a guy from one of those dating things. He had a deviated septum and squawked. And another through my hairdresser who had missing teeth and collected comics. That cured me."

"You can always visit me and watch the old bastards in their speedos."

As she stepped off the elevator she heard guttural moans coming from his room. "He's fine. He's just confused from the sedation." assured his doctor.

While driving home Mary suggested they stop at John's to pick up mail and get 'a lay of the land.' Although it was forbidden, the putrid odor of nico tine overwhelmed the apartment. In spite of its many windows and ornate crown molding the place seemed anemic.The furniture had belonged to his mother,Grace. In the living room stood two massive wing chairs in faded blue and orange brocade facing a non-functioning fireplace. A sagging sofa covered in a pale blue slip cover sat behind Grace's beloved inlaid coffee table. On top of it were scattered bills and two Bic lighters. Grace's Hummels adorned the mantle. The kitchen was orderly but atrophied. The counters and sink looked as though they had been swiped, not scoured. On the crusty shelves were a few bowls and plates that expected no one. Nancy felt a pang of sadness but remembered he lived in a college town brimming with activities and causes. Mary found a can of Kitchen Cleanser and cleaned the sink. Nancy started on the bathroom. As she wiped the tub with bleach she realized that in spite of efforts to cheer him he would continue Googling the latest catastrophes with a cigarette teetering on a nearby ashtray.

"You're in one of your reveries, Mom," said Mary as they drove back to her apartment. "He had a free choice." Her mouth folded into the shape of a cheery; the purveyor of common sense had spoken and the subject was closed. Frank was waiting in front. The three sat around the kitchen table pensive as they ate pasta.

"Should we talk about another place for him. Those stairs are a bitch for someone in his state."

"He would have apoplexy in one of those senior residences. He doesn't see himself as old .Tomorrow when we tackle those windows it'll look a lot brighter." said Frank

The following morning Nancy and her two children were sitting in Dunkin' Donuts looking peaked and frazzled with images of an endless dirge.

A pail stood outside John's apartment. Frank turned the key before he realized it was unlocked. A sound of clatter was coming from the kitchen. A glistening bronze body unraveled itself. They shook the hand of a woman who introduced herself as Valentina. She had a willowy body and reckless looking breasts that frightened Nancy. Valencia walked into the living room and sat in the wing chair as someone familiar with their surroundings. She had met John one day at a book sale. She was a widow and he was a "godsend." Nancy was feeling faint.

"He spends most of his time with me in Edison Park so of course the place looks neglected. He's a dear man," she took a sip from a Hello Kitty thermos. "I guess I fell in love with him." She whimpered. Frank went over and hugged her, pressing his cheek against hers.

"We are so happy to meet you."

Nancy suddenly felt they were treading on sacred ground and there was nothing to do but retreat.

"One more thing before you leave. I must be crazy but those old photos of your dad look like John F Kennedy."

The three sat in Starbucks silently reviewing the latest occurrence until their mother suddenly laughed. "That's a relief. I was beginning to think he was a figment of my imagination."

Chapter 10

Good Tithings

It is Sunday, two weeks before Christmas. Margaret (and that is what she emphatically insists upon being called) is at the reception desk of the Saint Frances Cabrini Shrine. She has been a volunteer there less than a month but already recognizes the usual gamut of the workplace, that mist of power and leverage that permeates wherever humans dwell, be it hallowed grounds. The director is a short feisty Hispanic nun who Margaret believes exploits both her stature and her accent. She watches Sister Alphonse ravenously tally the dollar bills from the donation boxes in front of the Saint's roped off death bed. She also witnesses an undeniable shift from solemnity to jocoseness when Sister Alphonse sees the Perpetual Prayer and Mass donation envelopes accumulate on the front desk. Margaret has just recently been assigned the task of counting and recording the money into a white leather journal.

Margaret's friend Lydia is waiting for her in the Chapel. Margaret hopes she won't come to the desk and want to be introduced. She is uncomfortable and anxious to leave. Especially now that a squeamish looking apparition has entered in gold lame pants and red turtleneck aglow in slivers of sequined martini glasses. Glenda's bluish hands are flailing dangerously near Sister Alphonse's eyes. She is a parched and puckered overwrought woman of indeterminate age who wears a horrifyingly cheery smile in spite of clearly been kicked to the curb a time or two. Today she has brought along her dog, Star, to show off his Xmas sweater. The nun is displaying uncharacteristic forbearance because Glenda is a fervent believer in Perpetual Masses. Today she discovered two pencils in the snow and is asking Sister Alphonse whether this is a Divine message. Margaret knew if Lydia heard any of this she would tell people about her friend's pitifully dull or as Lydia would put it "barren life". Margaret walked ahead of her friend as they proceeded to Clark Street.

"What's the hurry? I thought you loved that place?"

"I just wanted to get the hell out of there. That's all."

"Well I'm so famished I'm starting to get light headed. We can go to the Macy's Walnut Room and I'll use my credit card."

Lydia picked at her pasta, taking tiny bites as if somehow her daintiness would obliterate her weight gain.

"Oh damn! Why did I eat those peppers? They hate me!" Lydia complained as they strolled through cosmetics.

"I guess I better look at lingerie. I'm thinking of those one piece footie pajamas for Lisa. I certainly couldn't see her in a sexy nightgown but who knows what she likes? She is always on Facebook with those inspirational messages about sunshine and rainbows and kittens...damn those kittens!. And really to God. Who makes mother, daughter dresses anymore? But bless her heart. She means well."

Lydia stopped sniffing the Channel and grabbed a sample of hand cream from an elf.

"They're so.....you know...mother daughter dresses, scrapbooking and girl scouts. It's all so...Lutheran."

"Brian isn't Catholic anymore and you know it. He told me once he quit going to Mass in college," Margaret replied with relish.

"Stop! You're killing me. I try not to think about it. I sob listening to Adeste Fidelis, remembering him serving Midnight Mass at St Theresa's. Speaking of which, you've sort of outdone yourself in the Catholic department. Guarding shrines and all. I was telling June O'Malley about it and she thought maybe you were entering the nunnery. You once told her if you didn't remarry you'd become a Carmelite."

"I must have been in my cups when I said that so please set her straight for god's sakes! I greet people, sell prayers and Masses for the dead and pray for good vibes from St Frances Cabrini. You know like a miracle...a windfall of money or a man."

"Let me know if anything happens and I'll be there dusting the statues."

The elevator was clogged with earnest Midwest faces. Everybody was especially congenial, engaging one another in small talk and stepping out to let others off the elevator.

"Oh God, those peppers are wreaking havoc. I thought I was going to let one just when that lady was complimenting my coat. Wouldn't that have caused a stir?"

"They would have blamed the baby. You don't look like a public farter."

"Well, we're doing the escalator next time. Too much friendliness."

Lydia bought a stuffed toy called "Grumpy Cat" for her granddaughters. In lingerie she picked out a flannel onesie decorated in hearts.

"What's wrong, Margaret? Where's your holiday spirit? You haven't bought a thing."

"I go to Target for everything and my everything is almost nothing. I don't have much of a family except for my sister."

"Before I lose my mind with these crowds let's toddle on down to men's so I can get a sweater for my Brian."

The Men's department was complicated. The clothing was separated by designer instead of item which meant one could travel the equivalent of a city block in search of a sweater. Lydia was beside herself.

"Jesus, Mary and Joseph! Who wears some of this shit? Seventy- five dollars for a tee shirt with someone's ugly puss on it. Where are the simple navy blue V-necks? I hope I find the god damn sweater before I have a heat stroke and I wouldn't mind a little cocktail later and maybe split some calamari."

Margaret purchased Frango Mints before they left for the two block walk to Miller's Pub. Although Lydia minced behind her mumbling about her blocked gas she immediately grabbed for the basket of bread.

"What's going to become of us? You with your shrine and me at St Tim's rectory. I watch that show with that bitch who tells you how to handle money ..Susie something. I don't know what the hell these people are saying. They call up and tell her they got ten million in savings and a big ass house and different funds and shit I never heard of and they want to know if they can go to Mexico or someplace and she says something like 'you're not fluid enough.' What the hell's that about? I went to Mexico on a credit card the winter after Dennis died when I was losing my mind and guess what, Susie what-ever, I'm not homeless. So there. And this calamari will finish me off but tomorrow I start my new journey."

"Where in the hell are you going now?"

"Nowhere. It's my diet journey. I'm doing a new cleanse with watermelon and prunes."

Her diets were legion and always discussed over food.

"Oh for Chris sakes! Just cut down on your calories. Why do you have to be so dramatic?"

"You don't understand my metabolism, Margaret. You never have. So go ahead and pick a new subject as long as it isn't politics. You're being so quiet and you didn't buy anything but those damn mints."

"I don't understand your weight problems and you don't get my money problems. You say you don't have money but at least you're getting paid at St Tim's.

"Well, aren't you the life of the party! So you want to talk world problems? Well I don't because the whole damn world stinks. I watch the news and I get so nervous I have to snack. Terrorists are making me fat! Why can't everybody just sit the hell down and shut up. Give me a Jeopardy and Family Feud with my evening cocktail. My old brain can't take anymore crap. And those girls aren't going to like the stuffed cats. They probably haven't even seen the damn movie. They play with all those gadgets. Maybe I should take them back."

"I can't face Macy's again. I think we should call it a day," said Margaret.

The two slightly bent old women looked like hedgehogs huddled under the awning in black down coats. But they still saw one another as girls and perhaps that was one of the secrets to their abiding friendship. "Mind if I catch this next taxi?" asked Lydia.

"Not at all. I'm going to take the brown line. A taxi would break me."

"Merry Christmas. I love you!" both yelled simultaneously.

Margaret felt an immediate, almost erotic glow as she entered the apartment. The sizzling heat from the radiator and her cat, Max rubbing against her leg triggered a vague childhood carnality. She dutifully fed Max before pouring herself a generous glass of vodka. Though she referred to them as martinis her drinks were a splash of water, a generous slug of vodka and a few olives to give the appearance of restrained preparation. She called her sister, Pat who lived in Plantation, Florida and was surprised she didn't answer. Margaret made another drink over which to ponder her sister's whereabouts. Her thoughts turned to Lydia. They had known one another since the 60's while working downtown in Accounts Receivable at a small market research company. The friendship was founded upon an implicit negotiation; an exchange of compliments along with feigned interest in one another's romances. Lydia and Margaret met their husbands at a bar called McGuire's on Division Street. Butch McGuire took personal credit for these matches and photographs of couples lined the back of the bar. Lydia's life proceeded according to Butch McGuire's blueprint. She married Dennis, an Irish accountant. They had an apartment near Division and continued to visit "their" bar on Friday nights until they dutifully purchased a bungalow in Edison park and produced four children.

Margaret met Bill at McGuire's as well but Bill was a handful. One Saturday remains in infamy for Margaret. Her mother, Helen was invited to dinner. Bill was out of bed at dawn and buying groceries at the Jewel by seven. His levity made Margaret nervous. He scoured the bathtub and sink while singing along with the Temptations. He fussed over Helen, posturing as a waiter with a napkin over his arm as he poured her wine. But in the middle of Helen's account of her recent cruise to the Bahamas the phone rang and a woman asked for Bill. Margaret's lips withered along with her meticulously teased beehive. It took a few days but Bill finally admitted to having a girl-friend. She hadn't even had the satisfaction of flowers or late night phone calls begging for another chance.

After watching the news she listened to a concert by the Mormon Tabernacle Choir. She called these hymns her spiritual Viagra and had all kinds of epiphanies while listening to them. She thought about Lydia again and wished for a moment that she too had children. She read once in a science magazine that like animals, humans molt, only instead of fur they shed their skin. Margaret wondered if parenthood wasn't a kind of a molting as well, the shedding of that repugnant folly of certainty replaced with a bit of humility and compassion. She had to admit she was becoming as intractable and crusty as her mother's cast iron frying pan that sat unused on the back burner of the stove. She padded into her bed-room with her purse under one arm and her cat under the other. Her gnarled thumb and index fingers deftly retrieved from beneath makeup, a wallet and a pile of old receipts in a white envelope embossed with a crucifix. She lay the envelope on her bed. Next she pulled a plas-tic shoe container from the back of her closet and put it on the bedside table. She shook the envelope's contents into the box and with an imperious click she closed the box and returned it to the closet.

The next morning she remained in bed reviewing a dream in which she and Saint Mother Frances Cabrini were shopping in Macy's. Two opposing schools of thought were giving her a headache. She had left the T.V on overnight and a chirpy lady was giving unusual recipes for turkeys while the squabbling in her brain persisted. She managed a sitting position and while scratching her legs, momentarily pondered the flavor of taco stuffing. After cleaning the litter box and replenishing its food and water she cajoled her cat into bed and continued to ruminate. She arose suddenly with such a fury the cat leapt across the room. Once more she fetched the plastic box. She didn't bother with a bra. She pulled an old pair of L.L Bean ski pants over her flannel bottoms and grabbed an equally decrepit puffy down jacket whose feathers were escaping into the air like hatchlings. In the top drawer of her dresser she found a box of old Christmas cards decorated with kittens peeking out of pastel wreaths. On the envelope she wrote 'Merry Christmas'.

Ray's Market was almost empty but Regina was there. Regina who traveled over two hours each way to bag groceries and attend night school was at her post. Margaret purchased bananas and handed her the envelope. She had kept just enough money for Dunkin Donuts. The sun's reflection on the snow was dazzling. It made her feel giddy as she walked back towards her apartment sipping her coffee.

Chapter 11

Passion Play

On Monday at precisely six a.m. Sheila was staring at a popcorn ceiling in what she called her crypt but had been advertised on the internet as Hiatus Luxury Apartment / Homes in Davie, Florida. If she had been a comic book character there would be a bubble hovering by her head with a large "what happened? "in it. Sheila was prone to fretting and at any given moment she had her choice of an emporium of topics. This morning she chose a disturbing theory that had taken form around two a.m. Contrary to a lifetime of Catholic dogma Sheila was starting to question the idea of free will. The idea of a preordained life was making more sense by the year. Nothing else could have explained some of her decisions.

As a teenager she had lived ten miles east of her present residence. Following a lengthy hospital stay for a bleeding ulcer her father had taken early retirement from teaching high school and moved the family from Chicago to Hollywood, Florida. Her older sister, Clare loved Florida from the moment the two girls stepped off the Seaboard Express. Sheila could not fathom how someone with the same genes could have such a contrasting view of a place. Clare was content to go to the Hard Rock Casino once a week. Now, as an older adult it was disturbing to see her flesh and blood at Bud's Deli on Monday mornings exuberant in a pastel top with buttons in the shape of martini glasses. She felt as betrayed as if her sister had left the Catholic Church and joined a snake worshipping cult in Althea, Florida. The previous winter Clare somehow convinced Sheila to leave Chicago where she had been living since graduating from college forty years ago. Clare owned a condo at Flamingo Lakes in Davie. Sheila remembered Davie as a dusty little town known solely for its rodeos but her sister assured her that this was now the "smart place to live." After settling in, Sheila began to question what that meant. No one looked that smart as they shuffled around malls in a heat induced torpor. Clare had also described Davie as centrally located. But to what? Sheila had sold her car to her downstairs neighbor because it never occurred to her urban sensibilities that any place outside of a third world country lacked sidewalks and reliable public transportation. There was a shuttle bus advertised as "just steps from her front door." Minerva the Haitian driver would stop at Publix Foods to weigh herself leaving her passengers to listen to piped-in Christian music.

Like dogs left in a car they would scratch themselves and stare anxiously out the window looking for signs of Minerva. But Sheila consoled herself with the idea that writers are vampires feeding off such characters and Sheila called herself a writer.

Sheila joined a writing workshop at the library shortly after moving to Davie. The moderator was a crusty guy in his sixties with a gray ponytail and a few published essays about his teaching days in the Bronx. She figured that Hank Frankel had every right to be cranky. Instead of regaling New York with his talent he was living off the fees of mediocre writers at a branch library in Davie, Florida. The majority came only long enough to read their excruciatingly unfunny anecdotes or funnier attempts at serious memoirs. The deal was to listen so you would be listened to. Praise and you will be praised except for Hank who was heaving with vitriol. Sheila kept coming back because most of Hank's critique was valid and she empathized with him. Back in her Chicago apartment she had pictured engaging a select group of local writers with her droll observations like another V.S. Pritchett. But she was a dreamer and she knew that dreamers after thirty are annoying. Her pragmatic Irish mother would have said that "Sheila is going off halfcocked." She had started writing a book of short stories that were mostly about Florida. Hank said the writing wasn't bad but the context liked vitality. And he was right. There were no crescendos. The stories were like sickly waifs, puny and unadoptable.

"Writing is not some flimsy notion. A short story is a craft with a beginning, middle and end. The writer has to corner the reader like a carnie guy and a really great writer will infuse the reader's soul, transforming him from a fan to a disciple. That's if you are a true writer. But you have to be that carnie guy. No writer is beyond technique and ploys. Keep your fancy proclamations under wraps. Let the reader find his own." Frank had paused for a second and added with a snarl "Of course most people read pure crap."

Sheila loved him for his candor but not everyone did. Joyce Praker waddled out in a huff with her manuscript tucked into a Hello Kitty backpack. Her story involved aliens, Elvis, and John F Kennedy whom they had somehow revived and were using as informants. Sheila continued to make the weekly trips but that cold intractable blueprint of the short story remained elusive.

The subject of money and employment had eventually become a serious issue. No one seemed to care whether Sheila read classics or had, as she so pitifully clung to, the gift for writing. She'd only been in Davie a few months when she realized that unless she sold drugs, food or real estate the job market was bleak. She was feeling particularly desperate one afternoon when, after purchasing allergy pills and Q-tips she filled out an application at Walgreen Drugs. Later that evening while sipping a martini and listening to Bach on her "Micro Fiber Sunset Red with easy financing" couch that she had giddily purchased at Ocean View Furniture for 29%

percent interest, she realized with what could aptly be called a conniption fit that she could not under any circumstances listen to Evelyn, the numbskull cashier talk about her dimwitted boyfriend, Slade and Precious, her Maltese every day.

She eventually landed a job at a children's museum, which was nestled between Walgreens and Lefty's bar. She had never associated a museum with a strip mall but by then she realized she was in a parallel universe. The owners, Jill and Bernice, a mother daughter team, resembled mob wives more than genteel mavens of the arts. Both women had imposing shades of red hair, skillfully sliced faces and tiny but impudent breasts. Like sandpipers they skipped around the various plastic huts and tents, sticky and dusty from accumulated spills of Juicy Juice, and calculated their days take while giving the socially prominent of Davie such as Amber Lipsky and her daughter Summer a peck on both cheeks.

In addition to reading the tabloids Sheila had a few other secret weaknesses. She was mesmerized by Reverend Dick Talbot from his Little Flock Baptist Church in Homestead, Fla. This was a guy who made scamming seem like a breeze. He would wipe his brow and squint as he looked out upon his congregation as well as his "generous TV audience." One evening looking straight towards her bed he made a pronouncement, "It is always darkest before dawn" in a hoarse anguished tone as an 800 number scrolled across the screen along with images of a Visa and MasterCard. This time the man on the pulpit in his silk Hawaiian shirt, linen pants and sun bleached pony tail would be right on target. Just when Sheila had decided to cut her losses, cash in her Roth IRA and return to Chicago she found a "real" job. St Timothy's Catholic school hired her as a permanent substitute teacher which assured her of at least three days a week. She found a ride with a second grade teacher Cyndi Tater who also lived at Hiatus and had told her about the job opening in their workout room. Every morning she was treated to the latest on Cyndi's daughter Cayce, who was first in Davies's junior gymnastic competition as well as runner up Little Miss Rodeo.

Humans are resilient and life takes merciful turns. She had a easy schedule and was calling Cyndi a friend within a few months. Catholic Grammar school had taken on a brighter hue than her days at St. Gertrude's in Chicago where it seemed as though she was always kneeling. If it wasn't First Friday it was some saint's day. In those days she had to fast in order to receive Holy Communion. At least one child would vomit or faint in their pew. Back In the classroom a musty smelling nun would toss glazed donuts and ice cold cartons of milk on the desks. She would be especially cranky because Mass had curtailed another in the series of God's harrowing earthly life. Sheila never again ate glazed donuts.

Everything else remained eerily unchanged. This was another testimony to her theory of a Grand Design. How else could she explain the fact that various species of children were so flawlessly dispersed? It was preordained that there would be prematurely ripe, hormonally challenged twelve year old girls who spent recess grabbing the boys. Most of the eighth grade boys however looked like they still happily fit on their mother's lap. But there were always a few tall ones with sprouting whiskers and strange voices who compensated for their freakishly untimely manhood by being class clowns. In second grade there's always the pudgy girl. She is grandma's playmate who can recite the menu at an Early Bird Special and her Brownie merit badges. Her male counterpart usually has a name as big as him. He'll circle the teacher's desk imploding with nervous prodigious conversation. Years ago he would be wearing a scapular. Sadly, there is always the ill-fated ragmuffin whose tee shirt and name could have been pulled from a bin. Every generation labels them differently but they are the same feral creature escorted through a lifetime of social services ; the bullies who get their seats changed every week. Neglect and despair are in their eyes. They beg for acceptance with brute force yet cling to one another like frighten animals. Staff rooms are equally predictable. There is always someone like Teresa Quigley and her infinite supply of bad tidings.

"We saw Bill and Kay O'Malley the other night. You know Kay from Altar Rosary don't you?" the question was directed at no one in particular.

"Anyway Bill wasn't himself and they left Poppin' Fresh right after dessert. God! and those cream pies are to die for. Well excuse the pun but that's what Bill did, so help me God. I heard from Kay's sister that he woke up about one a.m. and he said that he felt like shit and then he died right there in bed."

Sheila made valiant attempts at avoiding Theresa but sometimes it was just too much trouble. Sheila's own Irish family had seemed like they were counting the days until they were delivered from their earthly trials. Her mother with her novenas and rosaries was racking up grace like her MileagePlus for heaven. The Sullivan family however was not the dying type although they talked about it incessantly. They became increasingly morbid and toothless and lived in various back bedrooms until they withered away. Sheila's great grandmother smoked a pipe and drank more than a few generous shots of bourbon each week until she died at ninety- eight.

On this Monday morning Sheila had tried reaching the vending machine without being noticed. She needn't have worried. The teachers were radiant over Mrs. Quigley's news. Nancy Quinn was wearing a sweater embellished with twenty six bears each holding a letter of the alphabet. Her legs were dangling from the chair with her feet engorged in red ballet flats like frosting on cupcakes. Her dimpled fingers were daintily picking at a Dunkin Donut cruller.

"May he rest in peace. Kay will never be the same."

By the time the alarm went off at seven the following day the news had become repetitious. A tropical storm was heading towards South East Florida. Schools were closed so there was nothing to do to but listen to the governor and the local reporters discuss the storm. Their local weatherman, basking in the drama, had replaced his sport shirt with a somber suit. By late afternoon rain battered against the jalousies and the electricity went out. She was unprepared for its ferocity and sat in the corner of her tiny living room huddled in front of a battery operated black and white TV sipping Bota Box Pinot Grigio.

On Wednesday almost everything had returned to normal. The utilities were on and except for fallen branches the eye of Hurricane Katrina had spared them. Schools were still closed so Sheila and what seemed like all of South Florida were in Publix grocery store. Wild eyed shoppers were hugging one another in the aisles like rescued hikers. But the evening news was sobering. Katrina had taken a vicious turn. The feeder ban resembled a fetal monitor gone crazy as Katrina was swirling into the Gulf coast. Disaster was unfolding in monumental proportions like a Japanese science fiction movie.

Katrina was ravaging Louisiana. A levee broke and New Orleans was drowning. Throngs of people were lined up at a superdome waiting for refuge while others were on roof tops screaming for rescue. It was unfathomable that something this grotesque could happen in America. Supplies were not being delivered and people were dying. The sports arena had become a lion's den for the poor and a national embarrassment. The country's destitute were being exposed and politicians were fumbling for excuses like someone who'd left their baby in a hot car.

School resumed on Thursday. No one mentioned the Louisiana debacle. No one tattled. The trouble makers picked at scabs and drew distorted figures in black. The chubby girl was reading aloud from her social studies book but Sheila wasn't listening. She was looking out at the pasture next to the rectory where Father Quinn kept his donkey, Whisper and his horse, Patrick and thinking how seldom she and Clare got together.

"Where's Whisper?"

"He died" said one of the waifs looking helplessly at Sheila. "He was electrocuted in the storm."

At noon the children quietly gathered their lunches and marched to the lunchroom. Their little cubbies with the wrinkled papers and soiled sweaters had taken on the Divine quality of a saint's relics.

On Friday Sheila got to school early. She immediately went to the window. Patrick was barely standing. He was leaning against the fence with his head bowed. At lunch Sheila almost ran into the lounge. No one was talking. The Friday coffee cake was missing and Mrs. Quigley was frightfully subdued.

"Has anyone looked at Patrick this morning? Is he sick?"

Mrs. Quigley started to cry. "He isn't eating because of Whisper."

Sheila was witnessing grief incarnate in this little creature. She had never paid much attention to either animal although the children seemed to communicate with them, spending most of recess huddled by the fence. Sheila thought about the animals and like most people do, reverted back to herself. She had never had a real romance, that savage tango with its torrid ups and downs. But love was different. Love was deceptively monotonous and simple. Love was terrifying when you know it holds the cards. She called Clare. "We don't see enough of one another."

"You know my number. Just call. I'm always here for you, kiddo."

That night Sheila couldn't honestly say if she would stay in Florida but she was certain she would buy steak for two and she had her short story.